SECRETS OF A SILENT STRANGER

A HIWAY BOOK

SECRETS
OF
A SILENT STRANGER

by

RUTH HALLMAN

THE WESTMINSTER PRESS
Philadelphia

F
HAL
copy 2

Book Design by Dorothy Alden Smith

Published by The Westminster Press®
Philadelphia, Pennsylvania

PRINTED IN THE UNITED STATES OF AMERICA

Library of Congress Cataloging in Publication Data

Hallman, Ruth, 1929–
  Secrets of a silent stranger.

  "A Hiway book."
  SUMMARY: Clint believes summer at the North
Carolina beach will be dull now that World War II
is over until he discovers a young German sailor
hiding in the marshes.
  [1. World War, 1939–1945—Fiction] I. Title.
PZ7.H15469Se   [Fic]   76–13598
ISBN 0–664–32598–X

TO MY MOTHER AND FATHER, who always extended
the hand of friendship to anyone in need . . .
and
TO MY HUSBAND, who is the kindest person
I have ever known

SPECIAL ACKNOWLEDGMENT
to Peggy Hoffmann
and the Longview Writers
for their supportive criticism

CONTENTS

SECRETS OF A SILENT STRANGER

1

X MARKS THE SPOT

IF ONLY one other person had been in sight on that lonely strip of sand! Then Clint Jordan would not have been so scared when the man in rags rose up over the top of Jockey's Ridge. The boy was lying against the ocean side of the big sand hill, one hand rubbing Mickey's long black ears. Even the dog was caught by surprise. The wind from the ocean whipped away any scent of a stranger's coming near.

Dog and boy leaped up, startled, when the man loomed behind their heads.

"What do you want?" Clint blurted out.

The stranger stood silent and looked down at the boy. Stringy blond hair straggling around his shoulders and a wispy beard helped to hide the man's thoughts. No friendliness came into the icy blue eyes. Only the rapid rise and fall of his chest told Clint the ragged figure was even alive.

The boy looked quickly over his shoulder to see how far he was from the big old store by the sandy highway.

"Who are you?" Clint tried to keep his voice from shaking.

The man moved one foot in its dirty old shoe. Clint waited no longer. He whipped around and bounded down the sand hill. Faster and faster he raced, toward the safety of the old gray building.

Mickey raced with the boy as fast as his short legs would carry him. Clint did not stop to see how close the man was until he reached the bottom of the store steps. Mickey slid to a stop in a shower of sand and pebbles.

Only when his hand was on the door did Clint look back. Not a living thing met his eyes—low sand dunes covered with sea oats stretched gradually to the peak of Jockey's Ridge, more than a hundred feet up into the sky. And there was no one—no ragged stranger. Not one thing but sand.

Clint took a shuddering breath and plopped down on the porch under the sign: GENERAL STORE, A. B. WEATHERS, PROPRIETOR AND POSTMASTER, NAGS HEAD, NORTH CAROLINA. Panting, Mickey lay down beside him.

"Mickey, I didn't dream him up, did I? He was real— or sort of, wasn't he?" The boy laid his head on the dog, hugging him tightly.

The screen door behind them slammed, sending Clint and Mickey to their feet again.

"Boy, do you need a vacation! You jumped like a scared rabbit!" Herbie looked down with teen-age superiority at his younger brother. The grin on his face angered Clint enough to put some strength back in his shaky legs.

14

"I say, brother and dog, what's your problem?" Herbie grinned again.

"None of your business, Mr. Big Stuff! Where are Mom and Dad?" Clint demanded.

"Inside—and we're all tired of waiting for you. They only let you out at the sand hill for a short break while we picked up the key to the cottage. How come you were gone so long? Dad just sent me to look for you. What were you doing?"

Clint stared at his brother.

"Nothing—nothing that is any business of yours!" Clint brushed past Herbie into the dark coolness of the old store. He walked down the long room. High shelves of canned goods lined one side. Rows of dull brass mailboxes stood on the other side. Behind the cash register hung a calendar with a picture of a steam engine, smoke pouring from its stack. The date read July 1, 1946.

The store owner was talking to Clint's parents. He turned when he saw the boy coming.

"I've been waiting for you! I had to see if 1946 had made you or that black mutt any bigger! Can't say as another year has added much!"

"Hi, Mr. Weathers!" A happy grin lighted up Clint's face. "How've you been?"

"Well, I'll tell you," said Mr. Weathers. "When July rolls around, my whole summer gets brighter! Then I know the Jordans are going to be here again for vacation. Things can get mighty quiet in the winter months. But I do have something new to tell you this time. You, too, Mr. and Mrs. Jordan. We got us a mighty strange creature back in the sand hills. Came drifting up this winter like he crawled out of the quicksand. He's so creepy he makes me think he's nothing *but* quicksand."

"What do you mean, Al?" asked Clint's dad.

"Well, this man just turned up here one day in the oldest, torn clothes you ever saw. Don't know where in the world he found such rags. Don't have any idea where he came from. And never a word has he said. I reckon he just never learned to talk! But he brings me things he finds on the beach, chops some firewood for me now and then—and I give him what food he gets to eat. I guess I'm the only place he gets anything."

"Well, where does he stay, Mr. Weathers?" asked Clint.

"Don't have any idea! He always starts toward the Sound, then cuts across the sand hills toward that place where there ain't no cottages. Being so curious I took me a hike all over that area one day this spring. I couldn't find nothin' but sand, the Sound, and low trees. Couldn't see how anybody could be living round there—specially in the winter. Mr. Clint, I'll just let you and that runt of a dog solve the mystery of my stranger who don't talk. You've got a whole month to roam them hills and find out all about him."

"No, sir, Mr. Weathers!" said Mrs. Jordan sternly. "I've told my children never to get near strangers. One as peculiar as that man sounds is the very kind to stay away from. Do you boys hear me?" She looked at Clint as if she knew which one would worry her most. Clint knew he would never be allowed up on Jockey's Ridge alone if he told he had already seen the man in rags.

16

Keeping the news to himself seemed the best idea for now.

"Here's the key to the Jackson cottage, Mr. Jordan." Reaching up on the shelves behind him, Mr. Weathers handed over a big key. "Hope you folks will have a real nice month."

"Thanks, Mr. Weathers." Turning to his family, Mr. Jordan said, "Last one outside is a rotten elephant! Come on, let's make our summer magic now."

Herbie shook his head.

"He feels he's getting too old, Ed," said Mrs. Jordan. "But you and Clint go ahead and have your fun."

"Come on, buddy!" Dad said to Clint. "We know what magic can do, don't we!"

The two of them raced outside to the sand by the porch steps. Clint watched his father draw a big circle, putting a large X right in the middle.

"Okay, it's up to you, Clint. If you can spit to the center of the X, you'll make it the best summer ever. Keep your toes back of the line and ready—one, two, three!"

Bingo! Right slam in the middle! And no wonder, because Clint had been spitting in circles all winter. Nineteen forty-six had to bring the best July ever.

The Jordan family climbed into their old gray car and headed for the cottage. Clint wondered if the tall, silent man was this summer's special magic.

2

ROOFTOP PRISONER

CLINT DIDN'T WORRY about splinters as he raced down the long wooden walk leading over the water to the Jackson cottage. With Mickey at his heels he ran all around the porch that framed the little house. He had to inspect his territory.

Everything seemed okay. The porch railing was still rickety, but Clint had learned long ago not to lean on it. The back steps which led right down into the water had not been hurt by the winter's high tides. Mom and Dad could still push off from the steps in the little rowboat for some fishing. Clint sometimes went along with his pole, but he would rather jump off the porch and swim around or float on an inner tube.

Clint leaned under the railing to see if anything interesting had drifted against the pilings under the cottage. He looked back up just in time to see his older brother creeping up on him.

"There you go, fungus face!"

With one big push Herbie sent Clint tumbling into the

18

water. The older boy grinned down at his brother. Clint grabbed for the bottom step, but his brother kept pushing his hands away.

"Quit it! Quit it!" yelled Clint.

Mrs. Jordan came hurrying around the corner of the cottage.

"Boys, I am not going to have a whole month of you two fussing and teasing. Your father has some peace away from school and he does not want to hear children yelling all day long! Now, both of you come and help unload the car! This minute!"

Clint climbed out and the boys raced down the narrow little bridge to the car. Mr. Jordan loaded their arms with blankets, pillows, and sheets.

"Here, take these to the bedrooms and get those beds made up. And hurry! I'm hungry enough to eat seaweed raw and you know your mother won't take pity on me until she thinks we are halfway settled!"

As Clint and Herbie tromped off, Clint looked over the three-room cottage. It looked like an old barge tied up at the end of the narrow bridge.

First came the front bedroom, where Clint and Herbie slept—two iron beds, an old chest of drawers, nothing else to bother you. Next bedroom—same thing except there was a mirror over the chest of drawers. Mom and Dad slept there.

The kitchen was the best of all. A huge round table sat in the middle of the room surrounded by straight wooden chairs of every kind. Clint couldn't remember what the stove and icebox looked like, but they must be there. Mom's good food came from somewhere!

Clint didn't even mind his turn at helping with the dishes here because the window over the sink looked right out to the Albemarle Sound. Now and then he could spot a silvery fish arching out of the gray-green water.

That was the whole Jackson cottage. Yikes! No, it wasn't. He had forgotten the last room of all—and some days the most important. Tacked onto the left side of the weathered cottage was the outhouse, a two-holer to be exact. No modern bathrooms here. The cottage had been built too long ago.

Last summer that outhouse had been Clint's jail for almost a whole day. At least he had been lucky enough to be stuck on the roof instead of inside. It had all been Herbie's fault of course. With a brother like that what else could you expect! Clint's thoughts were cut off by a question from his mom.

"Clint, do you know where your father put the kerosene for the lamps?" she asked.

"No, I just have sheets and blankets."

"Ed, where did you put the kerosene for the lamps?" called Mrs. Jordan from the big kitchen. "It will be dark soon and I don't want to stumble around getting settled."

"Here, Herb, take this kerosene can to your mom," said Mr. Jordan as the boys came back to the car. "And help her get those lamps filled."

"Let me this time, Dad!" begged Clint.

"Next year, Sport, next year. I need you to help with these boxes. Right now I know better than to trust your brother with any type of food at all. I'm sure he has a couple of hollow legs where he puts all that stuff he eats."

His dad was something, Clint thought to himself. He

could make you feel like a giant in the world right at the same minute that he was refusing to let you do something he thought you were too young to do.

"Hey, Dad, you think this summer can ever be as good as last year?" Clint looked up at his dad.

Herbie let out a whoop as he passed by with the kerosene can, "You mean when you were trapped a whole day on the outhouse roof? You did it to yourself. You took my harmonica, didn't you, Creep? And you're so smart you dropped it in the water. You're lucky you are still in one piece!"

"All right, all right!" Clint shot his brother a dirty look. He turned to his dad. "I mean that coat I found last year on the ocean side of the island, the one with the funny buttons and that map in the pocket. You know, the map that showed all the inlets and harbors of the Outer Banks. You made me turn it in to the Coast Guard, remember?"

"Oh, yes." Mr. Jordan handed a box to Clint. "The officer in charge said they believed it belonged to the German spy they caught on the beach last summer. You claimed thinking about that coat kept you from going crazy when you were cornered on that roof so long!"

"Well, fungus face, I'll do more than corner you on a roof next time you take anything else of mine," said Herbie. "You'll never see daylight again!"

"Well, that was last year!" Mr. Jordan told Herb. "He had enough punishment staying up there all day. And he paid you for your harmonica doing jobs for your mom and me. Leave him alone, Herbie, I'm telling you. Let's get this work over and we can start having some real fun *this* summer."

Herbie knew from the steely tone of his father's voice that the matter had better be closed for good. Lugging the heavy kerosene can, he loped off to the kitchen.

And so another wonderful July began. Clint's glance roamed from the roof of the outhouse across the water to the sandy road and on to the towering shape of Jockey's Ridge. Nowhere on the Eastern coast was there a hill of pure sand as high as this one and its slightly lower sisters. He was too far away to spot anyone on the hill, but his thoughts drifted to the silent stranger he had seen earlier. Mr. Weathers had said the man did not talk at all. Clint tried to imagine how it would feel not to be able to say a word.

Mickey's barking snapped Clint out of his daydream. "Go get him, Mickey!" he yelled.

The little black dog was playfully chasing a sand fiddler at the edge of the water. This was his special summer fun. Now what would be special for Clint this summer? Certainly something better than a day clinging to the roof of the outhouse.

Carrying the heavy box of food, Clint pursed his lips in a whistle and set off around to the kitchen.

3

THE SEARCH FOR MICKEY

"ON YOUR FEET, boys!"

Mr. Jordan strode into the front bedroom just as the early-morning sun warmed Clint's face. Mr. Jordan looked like a beachcomber in his cut-off pants and bare feet.

Herbie groaned and pulled the pillow over his head, but Clint bounced out of bed. He could hear Mickey barking at something out on the sand.

"That black pup knows more how to enjoy a vacation than you boys. He's been chasing sand fiddlers since sunup—and half the night as well, your mom says. Now get a move on! We'll be ready to go get the water jugs filled as soon as you've had enough of Mom's pancakes."

Herbie struggled out of bed at the thought of food to fill the bottomless pit he called a stomach. Jumping into swim trunks, the boys were seated at the big kitchen table almost before their dad.

"Well, well—I kind of thought pancakes and syrup, sausage, and cold milk might open your eyes—or at least your mouths!'' said Mr. Jordan.

Mickey was at Mrs. Jordan's feet, silently begging his share. He let his tail talk for him.

When nothing was left on the plates but pools of melted butter and syrup, Mr. Jordan pulled the car keys from his pocket and said, ''Let's go. Time's a-wasting. We'll see you, Nell, as soon as we get the water jugs filled.''

Because the cottage had no plumbing, they had to get water from a pump back near the sand hills. Herbie didn't feel too old yet to miss the fun of riding on the front fender of the car for the trip. Going back into the sand hills to the nearest water pump was the only time their dad ever allowed this. He had to go so slowly over the thick sand road that he always let them ride on the front of the car.

Mickey raced along beside the car, barking at the turning wheels or at the boys' dangling feet. Mr. Jordan followed the winding road in and out between the low sand dunes. Soon they came up to the water pump in the shadow of towering Jockey's Ridge.

They took three ten-gallon glass jugs from the car. The water always tasted brackish, but it was safe to drink anyway. Clint usually held his nose to keep out the sulphur smell.

''Where's Mickey?'' Clint asked suddenly. The little black dog was nowhere to be seen or heard. Clint whistled his special call. Mr. Jordan looked up from his pumping to glance around the sand hills and low trees.

''Oh, he's probably found a sand fiddler to tease, Son, don't worry!''

"No, Dad," Clint said. "There are no fiddlers this far from the Sound and Mickey doesn't run off like that."

The boy turned all around, searching for his dog. He saw only the tall peaks of the sand hills sweeping up above him. On one side of him was the twisting road they had just traveled. In back stretched low yaupon bushes spreading out to the Sound that shimmered in the distance. That left only the marshy-looking area between Jockey's Ridge and the forest of low trees hugging the sand dunes to the north.

Mickey was nowhere in sight. Clint whistled again, but there was no familiar sound of the dog's jingling collar. The sun now seemed to press down on Clint.

"Dad, I can't wait. I've got to look for him."

"Son, he'll come back. He always does. But if you can't stand it, run on up to the top of the ridge. You can see all around from there. Just don't go near that marshy area. I don't know if it's really true that there's quicksand, but I don't want you over there."

"Oh, Dad, he's just trying to get out of his share of the pumping," growled Herbie.

"We'll give him another job later, Herbie," his father said.

Clint dug his feet into the soft, hot sand as he tore up the hill. Soon it became so steep he was digging in with his hands too. Panting, he turned to look down at his father and Herbie. They seemed like two tiny monkeys from so far up. Clint looked all around. Only sand, sea, and—silence faced him. No Mickey.

Then as Clint stood on the crest of the ridge, he cupped his hands and whistled. He heard one tiny yip! Frantically he tried to decide where the sound had come from. The best he could do was to guess where the dog was. But why hadn't he come at Clint's whistle?

The boy did not take time to yell to his father. He started at a tumbling run down the sloping sand hill toward the stretch of marshy land.

Clint went at such a fast run that he could not slow down. His leaps became longer and longer until suddenly he fell. Tumbling head over heels, he hit the level ground at the bottom of the hill in a spray of sand.

Clint lay still a minute to let the world stop whirling around. Slowly then he stood up, brushing the sand from his face and hair. When he could see once again, he looked around for Mickey.

Stretching out ahead were marshy patches leading up to the low trees and slowly rising dunes some distance away. It was hard to tell which spots of sand were hard and which were soft and mushy. Like his father, Clint had always heard there were dangerous quicksand holes on this side of the hill. There were also whispered legends of an old Indian graveyard. Not even Herbie had wandered over this way.

"Yip-yeow-yip!"

That was Mickey's call for help! Forgetting the quicksand and the graveyard, Clint ran toward the sound from the little dog. His legs were scratched as he tore through the stiff saw grass. One foot sank into thick sand. Clint frantically pulled his foot out, with a sucking sound from the wet ground. The sand slithered together again, hiding its danger.

26

When Clint felt some firm ground under his feet, he stopped to listen again. Where was Mickey? This time he heard scratching noises. He looked all around. At first he saw only waving clumps of saw grass. Then he looked at the first dune rising near him.

Heavy clumps of grass were growing all over the dune except for one spot where some old boards were lying. From this spot came Mickey's cry for help one more time.

"Yip!"

Clint leaped across the wet sand toward the dog. He was almost on top of the old boards when an eerie feeling made him stop. These old boards covered something. Clint dropped down on the sand and stared at them. What was this place? In his mind flashed a picture he had seen in a book of Indian burial places. Sometimes Indians were buried in a sitting-up position to make their trip to the Great Spirit easier. Was this mound of sand hiding a grave? Had Mickey fallen into a tomb?

Clint inched his way toward the dune. He pushed a board with the tip of one finger. Unexpectedly it fell clattering inside the opening. Mickey yelped and tried to jump out. Clint was glued to the sand, waiting for something to happen. There was not a whisper from inside. After a minute Clint wormed his way up to the edge of the boards. He peered in. In the glare of the hot sun he could see this was no grave. But what was it?

He found himself looking back into a little cave. The walls, the floor, the roof were all made of old boards like the battered planks sometimes washed up on the beach. Mickey must have been snooping around and fallen down the one deep step between the boards. The little dog could not climb out. Clint sneaked one foot in beside Mickey, then the other foot.

The room was so small he could almost touch the walls from the middle. The top of his black hair brushed the roof. With the sun lighting up the little room, he could see plainly. Somebody—or something—lived here!

A half-burned yellow candle sat on a small table made from the same old boards. A cot like those in the beach cottages was on one side. It was covered with a mildewed old mattress so dirty it might never have been any color. The odor crept into Clint's nose. Only the hot sun shining in on his feet kept him from feeling he was in a cold, clammy grave.

This was certainly not a hideout that children had made. This was the kind of place only a grown-up could make.

All was cleverly hidden by the waving clumps of grass above. No one would see this place unless he was right on top of it—or unless he had a curious nose like Mickey's. And people didn't wander over to this marshy side, since it was not very welcoming.

Who could live in a cave like this? Who would need such a secret place? Clint shivered again. He felt clammy dampness creeping around him. Suddenly he realized the danger he and Mickey were in. If a person had so much to hide that he would live in such a dungeon, what would he do to someone who discovered his secret?

Clint grabbed Mickey and scrambled out of the hideaway. He stopped just long enough to place the boards back as he had found them. He took a look around and

28

started a stooping run across the marshy sand, his hand tight on Mickey's collar. When he was halfway to the bottom of the hill, he froze.

Starting down from the highest point of the ridge was the same ragged man he had seen the day before. The stranger was walking slowly down the sand hill.

Clint flattened himself right down into the sand. He let the tall saw grass close over him. With his hand tight around Mickey's muzzle, Clint whispered in the dog's ear.

"Not a sound—do you hear? Not a single sound!"

Clint did not know where the man was heading. Had he seen them? Was he coming for them? Clint held his breath and listened for the sound of the man's steps swishing through the grass.

They waited—where was the man? Had he seen Clint? Wait! They heard the soft sound of boards scraping together. For a few minutes more the boy waited with his head down, his hand tight on the dog. Then slowly he parted the grasses and peered toward the sand dune. The man was out of sight. The only place he could have disappeared into so quickly was the cave in that sand dune.

Very, very slowly Clint and Mickey half crawled, half ran across the marsh. He did not dare go up the hill and over to the other side where his father and Herbie were at the pump. He would have to take the long way around the base of the hill for safety. When he felt they were far enough away from the hideout, Clint bent double and ran as fast as he could, still holding on to Mickey's collar. He was afraid the dog would go back to investigate further.

29

When they finally came in sight of the pump, Clint let the dog go. Mickey ran barking to the little car where Mr. Jordan and Herbie were just putting in the glass jugs.

"Creep, count on you!" growled Herbie. "You sure can time things perfectly. How did you know we were through!"

Mr. Jordan said, "I was getting worried. Glad you found Mickey though. Did he give you a good scare?"

"Uh—yes—uh—"

Clint couldn't say why he did not want to tell anyone, even his dad, where he had found Mickey. He was not so scared now that he was back at the car. The silent stranger was his puzzle—and he was going to figure it out by himself. He and Mickey, that is!

4

THE MYSTERIOUS COAT

IN A FEW DAYS Clint was back on top of Jockey's Ridge. This time he was meeting his friend, Jud, for a picnic supper. Clint brought the peanut-butter-and-jelly sandwiches, potato chips, and some of his mother's famous brownies. Jud was to bring cola and marshmallows. After their supper the boys would meet Jud's mother at the bottom of the sand hill and ride back to spend the night at Jud's cottage on the ocean side.

Clint always liked staying at Jud's. They shared a first-floor front bedroom. The bedspreads and lamps had anchors, sails, and all kinds of fancy seagoing designs. And there was a real bathroom—modern enough to have a john you could flush. Best of all was the fun Clint and Jud had late at night. They would sneak out of the windows onto the porch and down to the cool, damp sand. They would stretch out behind a sand dune—watch the stars, gaze at the ridge of phosphorous in the crest of each crashing wave.

"Hey, Clint!" Redheaded Jud came clawing his way up

31

the last few feet to the razor-edged peak of Jockey's Ridge. Behind him crawled a boy whose shock of red hair made Jud's look like a pale sunset. "This is my cousin, Buzz, from Asheville. He's staying with us a few days."

"Hi, Buzz!" Clint looked at the bag in Jud's hand. "Did you bring the marshmallows and cola?"

"Sure. Found some dill pickles too. Did you bring the brownies?"

"You bet!" was Clint's answer.

The boys made a little ledge of sand with their hands and spread out their feast. Against their backs the sand was warm. The late afternoon sun tipped the hills with salmon pink.

"Hey, Clint, I sure am glad you finally got here." Jud grinned. "Now we can plan some really great days."

"I don't think anything can beat last year," Clint said.

"You mean that day you spent on top of the outhouse? Buzz, you ought to hear about that!" Jud rolled in the sand, laughing at the thought of Clint hiding from Herbie.

"Heck, no! Not that," Clint protested. "You know I'm talking about our finding that coat on the beach. I just wish they hadn't made us turn it in to the Coast Guard. I wish we had seen the Coast Guard capture the German who landed secretly right on our beach. Golly, that was some night! We nearly missed it all 'cause you wanted to stay inside and play cards."

"Yeah—and then we heard that gunfire. It sounded so close to the cottage I thought we'd get shot climbing out the window to the sand dune."

"You heard guns!" Buzz exclaimed. "Did you go out on the beach!"

32

"Heck, yeah! We were always out on that beach—even after the Coast Guard began patrolling on horseback every night," Clint said.

"And those guards were supposed to shoot first and ask questions second if they saw anyone on the beach after dark. But we slid through the sand just like soldiers. And we hid behind the clumps of sea oats on the sand dunes. They never even saw us!" bragged Jud.

"Yeah—but what happened that night you heard the guns?" Buzz asked.

Jud said, "Clint nearly got us in trouble! He got so excited he opened up those heavy blackout shutters on the window without turning out the light. Remember when World War II was still going on last summer? People living on the coast could not let any light show from the front or sides of their houses. We had to close those heavy shutters at sunset so no light could be seen by enemy ships or submarines at sea. And *no one* was supposed to be on the beach after dark."

"But we went on the beach nearly every night," said Clint.

"I think you were stupid!" muttered Buzz.

"Anyway—there was a lot of yelling and scuffling down on the beach after the gunshot. We got behind the sand dunes as quick as we could," Jud said.

"What did you see?" Buzz's eyes shone excitedly.

"At first we couldn't see anything. That night was black as tar! One man yelled that he had found a little rubber raft pulled up on the sand. The other man went back to the Coast Guard Station to report what had happened, remember, Clint?"

33

"Yes—then the Coast Guard officer came with some more men. He ordered them to search the sand dunes to see if there was anybody else around!" Clint was breathing hard.

"Did they find any spies?" Buzz asked.

"We didn't know until the next day they had captured one man right when we heard that first gunshot. And we had to hide almost all night because the Coast Guard kept searching. We sneaked up under Jud's front steps and tried to watch what was going on," said Clint. "Boy, were we tired when we finally got to bed! But we still got up early to see what we could find in the daylight. That beach was a mess of footprints wherever the tide hadn't already washed up. We climbed every low dune in sight. And then I found that coat right next to Jud's cottage."

"You mean *we* found that coat!" interrupted Jud.

"Uh-huh, well, anyway, we climbed over the dune right next to the steps where we had hidden, and there it was, rolled into a ball and stuffed in a clump of sea oats. It had a map in the pocket with words we couldn't even read. But whoever it belonged to must have been hiding right next to us!"

"Boy, I wish I'd been there," breathed Buzz. He looked at the other two as if they had captured the spy alone.

The first chilling breeze of the night swept over the three boys. They shivered—a little from memory, a little from the breeze. The year in between vacations had brought peace back to the shores of both America and Germany. Lights now began to glint in a few of the cottages spread out below them.

34

Jud put a match to the canned heat he had brought for their marshmallows. With shortened coat hangers they browned and burned marshmallows and ate them until they were stuffed like flounders.

"I wonder if they ever caught anybody else last summer?" Jud asked.

"Well, I never heard anything else about it. Course, I never read the newspaper much," said Clint.

"Me, neither!" said Jud, smiling. "Still that coat had to come from somewhere. And we'd have known if they had ever found anybody else, don't you think?"

"I guess so," Clint said. He glanced around from their perch on the ridge of the sand hill. Just yesterday he had tumbled down the north side in search of Mickey. His eyes roamed over the clumps of saw grass—the wet sandy spots. Nothing moved out on the marshy land— nothing human. He turned to look at Jud.

"Jud—I—uh," started Clint.

He couldn't say any more. He didn't know why. First he couldn't talk to his dad and now not to his best friend. Boy, he must be going kooks or something.

Jud was looking at Clint.

"Well, what? You got something to say, say it!" Jud scowled.

"Uh, nothing—just nothing—that's all." Clint looked away from the direction of the hideout.

"Well, we've got to go anyway," Jud said. "Mom's going to drown us all good if we don't get on down to the highway. If the wind's not blowing the right way, the mosquitoes are going to eat her up."

The three boys gathered up the picnic scraps and

35

stuffed everything in a paper bag.

"Geronimo!" yelled Jud as he started a leaping run down the hill.

Buzz slid down after his cousin.

Before starting his run, Clint paused at the crest of the ridge—shivering because of the cool night wind, shivering because of the secret hideout staring up at him from the gray shadows of the marsh, shivering because of the silent stranger.

He plunged down the hill after his friends.

5

THE TIGHTENING BELT

AFTER THE PICNIC on Jockey's Ridge, Clint spent the next three days in his own cottage. A northeaster, full of gusty wind and driving rain, blew in from the ocean. Storms never bothered Clint. They were just as much fun as the long sunny days.

He loved to stand out on the porch and let the rain plaster him. The ocean was so rough he could hear the roar all the way to the Sound side. But when the storm had passed, the sky, the beach, the old cottage, glistened in freshness. Clint woke up that third day to the soft lapping of the water against the pilings under the cottage. It was so early that Mickey had not yet started pestering the sand fiddlers. The dog was stretched out on the floor between the two beds.

As quiet as an eel Clint slithered out of bed, pulled on his swim trunks, and slipped out to the porch. Mickey softly pattered after him to the steps leading to the beach. Clint sat down for a talk with Mickey.

"Old buddy, first we'll take ourselves a little swim.

Then I think we should just stroll along the shore till we get near the sand hills. Maybe we can find out something about that man. It's time we put up or shut up—either find out about him ourselves or tell Dad something's fishy!''

He hopped up and ran down into the water. Holding his arms out like a flying fish, again and again he fell into the water. For a while Mickey jumped around with him. Then the little black dog wandered back to shore to sniff out a sand fiddler.

Soon Clint had had enough splashing. He started off through the shallow water toward a little cove near the base of the sand hills. Picnickers used this spot many times, but at this early hour Clint and Mickey had it all to themselves. When they reached the little cove, the boy sat down at the water's edge. He watched the little sand fleas dig their bubbly holes after each shallow wave. Some didn't make it quickly enough and Mickey had fun pushing them around with his nose. He never hurt them or Clint would have popped him good.

The boy stood up and stretched his brown arms. The towering sand hill behind him slept quietly in the early morning. He wondered if the silent stranger slept, too, on the narrow cot in his hideout. Clint knew he was afraid of the man—not only because of his strange silence. A person would not go to so much work to make a hideout unless he had some big reason for staying away from people—and that unknown reason scared Clint.

Clint knew why Mr. Weathers, the postmaster, had never found the hideout. As well as the danger of the marshy ground in that area, there had always been that tale of the Indian graveyard somewhere around those low dunes. Some people were superstitious and never went near those low mounds. Herbie laughed at Clint for believing in the tales.

Clint stared toward the spot where the man had built his hideout. If he could sneak up closer and keep watch on the place, he might learn something about the man. It was time to make a try. He walked back into the water to rinse the sand off his legs and arms. He walked out until the water reached his knees. A sharp shell or something he stepped on in the water made him stumble. Then he went on out a little farther. When he leaned down to cool his face in the water, he stared in puzzled surprise at the pink color swirling around him.

Further away from his own spot the water was its usual sandy color. Clint lifted up his feet, one at a time, trying to figure it out. When his left foot came up out of the water, he knew the pink color was his. Blood was pouring from a deep V-shaped cut on his heel. The boy felt a little sick as he saw how fast the cut was bleeding. A trail of pink led back to the spot where he had felt the sharp shell or broken bottle.

Clint didn't know how long it took to bleed to death, but he knew he was badly hurt. He was too far away from any of the cottages to yell for help. He didn't move because he couldn't figure out what to do.

Suddenly Mickey started barking frantically. First he raced to the water's edge—then back to Clint—then toward the cottages slumbering in the distance. All at once he stopped his rushing around and began to back away from a group of trees and bushes growing close to the shore. The hair along the dog's back stood up. A low growl came from his throat.

Clint looked toward the bushes. As he watched, the branches slowly parted showing the face of the silent stranger. The boy stood dumb—holding the foot from which blood was rapidly flowing. For just a second man and boy stared across the water at each other. Then in one quick move the man stood up, towering above the bushes. Rapidly he pulled his belt out of the loops on his tattered pants. Clint could only wonder in fright what the man meant to do. The stranger splashed toward him. Mickey made a leaping dash through the water to the man.

"Halt, kleiner Hund, halt!" commanded the man. Clint stared in amazement at the sound of the man's voice—at the gentleness of what sounded like an order —and at Mickey's sudden and complete obedience.

The man looked down at Clint. With the belt in one hand he reached for the boy. Clint was too afraid to back away, but there was no need. The man gently lifted the bleeding foot. Quickly he tightened the belt around the boy's leg, turning the leather strap tighter and tighter, until suddenly the bleeding stopped!

The man pointed toward the cottages in the far distance, then he pointed at Clint. The boy stared at the stranger. Again the man pointed to the cottages, then to Clint.

"Yes, yes!" said Clint, suddenly realizing the man was asking where he lived. "Oh, yes!"

Turning his back and bending down before Clint, the man motioned for the boy to climb onto his back. Clint

40

jumped aboard and grabbed the man's neck and they quickly set off for the cottages.

Mickey jogged along behind. He had never made a single growl after the stranger spoke to him. Or had the man really spoken? Were those words he had said, or just the sounds of a person who had never learned to talk? It had sounded like "halt" or something.

Suddenly the man stopped and gently lowered Clint to the sand. He lifted the boy's cut foot and loosened the belt. When the cut began to bleed, the man tightened the belt again and set off for the cottages.

Clint remembered from a first-aid book the rules for applying a tourniquet to stop bleeding. If the tourniquet was not loosened every now and then to permit the blood to flow, the foot could be permanently damaged from lack of blood. The man stopped two more times to loosen the belt before they reached the Jackson cottage.

Over the stranger's shoulder, Clint saw Herbie sitting on the steps of the narrow bridge, moaning out a song on his new harmonica. Herbie looked up at the man jogging toward the cottage with a bloodstained Clint on his back. Mickey began to leap around the older boy, furiously barking the news. Herbie's mouth gaped open, then he raced over the bridge yelling, "Dad, Dad! Clint's hurt bad and that dirty old stranger's got him! Hurry! Clint's bleeding all over the place!"

In a second Mr. Jordan had raced out of the cottage and was holding Clint in his arms. The stranger sank down on the sand, panting for breath after the long run with the boy on his back. His shirt was wet with sweat and blood. For just a minute he lay there. Then he struggled to his

41

feet. Pointing to the little gray car parked by the bridge, he began to pull Mr. Jordan to the car. Then he pointed to the tourniquet on Clint's leg.

"Quick, Herbie, get my car keys. The man is right. We must hurry! Clint needs a doctor. He's losing too much blood."

In two minutes the Jordans were heading for Manteo, the nearest town with a doctor. Mrs. Jordan held Clint close and for once he did not mind. His foot was throbbing and he felt dizzy.

The doctor in Manteo said someone had certainly saved the boy's life by applying the tourniquet, for an artery had been cut. With gentle hands he stopped the flow of blood and stitched up the cut. He gave Clint a tetanus shot to prevent infection and another shot to ease the pain.

Clint sat between his mom and dad all the way back to the cottage. He was half asleep when his dad lifted him from the car. Through half-closed eyes he saw his silent stranger waiting on the steps.

"He'll be all right," Mr. Jordan said. "You saved his life. We can never thank you enough. Please, won't you come in?"

Although he did not understand a word Mr. Jordan said, the man smiled his relief at seeing Clint. He would not go into the cottage. He turned back toward Jockey's Ridge, giving Mickey a pat as he walked past the dog.

"Oh, what a shame he cannot talk!" said Mrs. Jordan, looking gratefully after the man.

"But he can!" mumbled Clint. The boy spoke so softly no one heard him. "He can!"

6

A SECRET WORD

CLINT SLEPT the rest of the morning on a cot his father had set up in the kitchen. The shot the doctor had given him made him very drowsy. Late in the afternoon he finally began to wake up. To his amazement he saw Herbie sitting beside the cot. He knew his brother had not realized he was awake.

Suddenly Clint let out an Indian yell that sent Herbie straight up in the air. When the older boy saw the wicked grin on his brother's face, he stomped out of the room. He was furious with himself for having shown any concern for his fungus-face kid brother.

Mr. Jordan had seen the whole thing. He said, "See there, Mother, Clint's going to be perfectly all right. Everything's right back to normal!"

Clint started to get up from the cot.

"Oh, no, you don't move!" said his mother, hurrying over to push him back. "The doctor said you were to keep that foot up for at least three days. You stay right there."

"Here—on this cot for three whole days! I might as well be in jail. What a dumb way to spend July!" Clint turned to look at the wall so no one would see the tears filling his eyes.

"Let him alone, Mother. He'll have to accept it. He is lucky that stranger found him in time. Son, it's up to you how you take this—what kind of a boy you are. We'll start off by playing a game of hearts with you right after supper. Okay?"

Clint nodded but kept his face turned to the wall.

"You must be starved! You slept right through lunch." Mom hurried around fixing a tray for Clint. He had to sit up when she put the food down before him. And he had to admit he was getting royal treatment—cola, french fries, a cheeseburger, and fried applejacks rolled in sugar, hot and crispy—all Mom's way of saying she was sorry he was hurt.

Clint began to laugh a little when he listened to Herbie arguing about doing the dishes. Lying on this dumb cot might not be too bad if Herbie was going to have to do Clint's jobs as well as his own.

When the supper dishes were cleared away, even Herbie agreed to play cards with the family. It turned into a pretty good night. Clint never was caught with the queen of spades—the worst card in the game. His dad was nearly always the loser. And Mr. Jordan had fun pretending to lose his temper every time he was caught with the bad cards. Once he threw his cards all across the room. Clint nearly fell off the cot laughing.

Soon everyone had had enough and only the sound of water lapping against the pilings of the darkened cottage was heard. Just before he fell asleep, Clint remembered how he had felt when the stranger had started toward him with the belt in his hand. And then the gentle touch of the man's hands on his foot, the command to Mickey, or was it a command? His eyes closed with that last thought.

The first day on the cot had not been too bad. Clint had spent most of that day sleeping. The second day was a little harder, but a visit from Jud cheered him up. They had a game of checkers going for about two hours until Mrs. Sawyer came for Jud.

By suppertime, though, Clint was getting desperate for something to do. He begged Herbie to play a game with him, but his brother had lost interest in such a lively invalid. All Herbie was willing to do was bring to the cot a pile of old books he had found in the chest in their bedroom. Every beach cottage had a few ancient books lying around. The books Herbie found for Clint matched the advanced age of the old Jackson cottage.

Herbie went off to the sand dunes with some boys he had met. Mom and Dad couldn't be with Clint, because Mr. Jackson, the man who owned the cottage, had stopped for a visit. They were sitting out on the porch. So Clint was left to figure out his own amusement.

In desperation—and *only* in desperation—he picked up the books Herbie had dropped on the cot. The titles alone were enough to make a sick man sicker: *Introduction to Human Anatomy, Economic Principles, Problems, and Policies*—and something *real* exciting—*German Grammar Review*.

45

Clint leafed through the book on anatomy, hoping at least to find some grisly pictures of the human body. But whoever wrote this book seemed to care only about bones and muscles and junk like that. Clint tried the book on econo—whatever it was—but he could read only half the words in the first line.

Well, for no better reason except that the war with Germany had ended, Clint wearily picked up the textbook on German. He flipped through the pages, glancing at some of the English words with the German words right next to them. He was about to give up, when this summer's special magic began to slip into place. Right before his eyes were the very sounds—or words—that the stranger had made when he told Clint's little dog to get down!

The sounds the man had made were ringing in Clint's ears—*Halt, kleiner Hund, halt!*—They had to be the same! Clint's eyes flew to the English words right beside them—Stop, little dog, stop! Clint sat up on the cot so fast the book fell out of his lap. Frantically he grabbed it from the floor. Where was that page? He almost tore the book apart until he found the words again. This time he remembered the page number—92.

"Well, good night, Mr. Jackson."

Clint heard his father talking out on the porch.

"You be sure and come by again!"

His parents' footsteps echoed on the wooden porch as they walked back to the kitchen. He heard his dad call for Herbie.

"Coming!" was the answering yell from his brother.

Mom came into the kitchen to put out the kerosene lamp.

"Please, Mom—just a little longer. I want to read something!"

"Read! No, sir! You can do your reading tomorrow. You still have one whole day on the cot. You'll have plenty of time to read!"

"Mom—!"

Out went the light.

It was midnight before Clint's eyes finally closed. His thoughts tumbled over and over—*Halt, kleiner Hund*—Stop, little dog—the hideout—the man's fear of talking if all he could speak was German—the coat on the beach. Clint fell into a sleep as deep as the ocean. His mind was too tired for any more thinking.

The smell of eggs and bacon surrounded him when he finally woke the next morning.

Mom said, "I thought you'd never wake up. I've been banging pots and pans for an hour and you never stirred. You're getting to be a lazy old sleepyhead!"

When breakfast was finished and the kitchen was cleaned up, Mom said, "Clint, I'm sorry to leave you this morning. I have to go in to Manteo for some groceries. Dad has to go with me. Herbie will be around if you need anyone."

"Oh, that's okay—that's fine—I'll be fine—I mean okay!" Clint stumbled over the words in his relief that no one would be with him. He wanted to look at the German book by himself with no questions asked.

"You will? Be fine, I mean?" Mom looked at Clint in surprise. After all his begging for everybody to play with him, this was certainly a funny way to act.

"Well, anyway—you call Herbie if you want anything. Don't you dare get up yet." Mrs. Jordan took her pocketbook from the kitchen table and went out to the car.

As soon as Clint heard the car going down the road, he listened for his brother. He could hear the mournful sound of Herbie's harmonica out on the front porch. Clint pulled the German book out from under his pillow and quickly found page 92. There: *Halt, kleiner Hund*—Stop, little dog. Mickey looked up from his spot on the floor by the cot and wagged his tail as if he knew he was part of the mystery.

"We've just about got it, old boy!" Clint said to the dog. It had to be this way—the silent stranger *had* to be a German sailor who had landed on the beach last summer. The other German had been caught. The silent stranger had been hiding a whole year, pretending to be an American who could not talk at all. But the real reason he did not speak was because he would be caught and put in a prisoner-of-war camp. It had to be that way!

Clint lay back on the cot trying to make his thoughts clearer. Slowly he turned the pages of the book. He was trying to find something else—some German word he could learn to say that would trick the man into showing he understood German. Then Clint would know he was right. Near the front of the book in the easy words to say, he found it—the very thing, something easy for him to learn—*Danke*—thank you.

If Clint could just see the man again, he could say thank you—in German. Face to face he would know if the man understood.

Suddenly Mickey's ears perked up! The dog stood up

48

beside the cot, a low growl coming from his throat. Clint looked at the dog in surprise. Mickey wouldn't growl at Herbie or their parents. Just to be safe, Clint hid the German book under the pillow.

Again Mickey growled and padded to the kitchen door. Puzzled, Clint watched the dog. He was relieved to see the dog's tail suddenly begin to wag. When the silent stranger stepped through the door, Mickey was just one wiggle all over.

Clint sucked in his breath. He was too surprised to say anything. And he was afraid—of what he wasn't sure. The man had not hurt Clint when he had found him all alone in the water. He had been the one who had saved Clint's life. But now Clint knew who the man was—at least, he thought he knew—and he was scared to try his plan.

With only kindness showing in his blue eyes, the ragged man gently touched the boy's foot. Clint nodded in answer to the silent question as the man stooped down beside him. Slowly and carefully, from a bag in his hand, he took out his gifts and put them on the boy's pillow. There was a starfish perfect in every detail, a black devil's pocketbook shell, a conch shell whose pink matched the sunset on Jockey's Ridge.

The boy looked up from the gifts into the man's eyes. Swallowing hard, Clint softly said, *"Danke."*

The room was filled with a silence so frightening Clint could not breathe. But again the boy tried. *"Danke!"* he whispered.

The stranger slowly stood up, towering above the cot. Clint looked up in fear. But in the stranger's face was no anger—only a great weariness and a great loneliness. The man turned to the door.

"Wait, please!" Clint called.

As silently as he had come, the stranger was gone. The gifts on the pillow mocked Clint. Yes, the man was German. Clint had found out what he wanted to know and he was almost sorry.

But what now—what for Clint and what for the stranger?

7

BE MY FRIEND

TWO DAYS LATER Clint had figured out what he must do. Hobbling around as soon as his mom would let him, he began to gather the things he needed—paper, pencil, the German book, and some fried applejacks he had slipped from the kitchen. The one last thing needed for his plan fell into place early in the afternoon.

"Clint, Herbie and I want to go over to that old pier near the foot of the sand hills for some pole fishing. Why don't you come with us? You've been stuck around here long enough," Mr. Jordan said at lunchtime.

"Oh, do you think he should try something like that with his foot?" Mrs. Jordan began.

"Let me, Mom! You've got to let me!" pleaded Clint.

"The boy's ready to get out of prison," said his father. "Don't baby him. He'll be all right."

"Well—if you say so," answered Mrs. Jordan. She knew when Dad was acting like a superintendent.

With long bamboo poles sticking out the car windows, the three Jordan men set out on the same sandy road that led to the water pump near the high sand hills. Mr. Jordan hadn't even noticed Clint was wearing a shirt over his red swim trunks. Clint had to hide the things he had stuck in the waistband of his trunks. The floppy blue shirt covered up the bulges.

Mr. Jordan turned to Clint. "I haven't seen your stranger around since the day he brought you to us. Mr. Weathers said he hasn't even been to the post office."

The boy was so startled he didn't say anything. He thought wildly, He must have left! He's afraid he'll be caught and I'm too late!

"Too late!" he whispered to himself.

"What's that you said, Son?" asked Mr. Jordan.

"He's just mumbling to himself," said Herbie. "Three days on that cot have driven him loco—even crazier than usual!"

The little gray car stopped in the soft sand at the end of the road. The three Jordans got out with the bamboo poles, tackle box, and jug of water. Mickey danced around, eager to go anywhere, do anything. As Mr. Jordan started toward the path leading to the water, Clint said, "Uh, Dad—"

"What is it, Clint?"

"Uh—my foot kind of hurts. I think I'll just stay here awhile." Clint's throat felt as if it was closing on him for telling his father the lie, but he *had* to have some time alone here.

"Well, maybe your mom was right!" Mr. Jordan looked at him with a puzzled expression.

"I'll be fine. I'll rest awhile and then I'll come on to the pier and fish with you. I'll just take it slow and easy, but

I'll be with you after a while, honest!"

"Come on, Dad!" said Herbie, eager to get to the fishing.

Mr. Jordan made up his mind. "Okay, Clint. You can rest awhile here. But I'll expect you at that pier before too long, you understand?"

"Yes, sir."

Clint watched his father and Herbie going down the sandy path with the fishing gear. Mickey was in a spasm of eagerness to go to the water, but Clint's hand on his collar said no.

"I need you, Mickey, real bad!"

As soon as it was fairly safe, Clint headed off around the bottom of the sand hill at a fast hobble. He knew his foot would never let him take the shorter way over the top. Casting a longing look at the Sound, Mickey trailed his master. All the time Clint talked to the dog.

"You see, Mickey, you're the first part of the plan. You've got to try things out for me. I know he won't hurt you! You can't talk, but he knows I can tell. You've got to help me!"

When the boy and the dog came around the hill to the marshy area, Clint dropped down into a patch of saw grass. His foot was throbbing and he was hot and thirsty. Giving himself a minute to rest, he began to wiggle his way through the grass toward the low sand dunes. He wanted to see first—not be seen first.

He stopped and checked all around. It was a scorching day, with not even a trace of wind to ripple the grass. The hot July sun baked the whole island. Even the dull roar of the ocean's waves did not reach the spot today.

When Clint was as close to the stranger's hideout as he dared to go, he lay flat down on the sand. Pulling Mickey to him, he said, "Now, go, boy! Go find him for me!"

He gave the dog a little shove toward the sand dune. Mickey trotted off—black ears flopping. Clint watched the dog sniff his way up to the old boards lying on the dune. The dog pattered around, whining, scratching at the boards. Nothing moved. Clint had hoped so very much that the man would be spending this hot part of the day in the little cave. He watched through the grass as Mickey pawed at the boards.

Then, from inside the hideout, a hand moved one board aside. Mickey wiggled his hello all over. Very slowly the stranger put his head outside. He looked all around. Seeing no one, he began to rub the little dog's head. Over the sandy stretches came the sound of the man's voice as he started to talk to the dog.

Suddenly the man put his head down on the dog's back. His shoulders were shaking. Clint sat up in his clump of grass, surprised. Was the man crying—a man, crying! Getting to his feet, Clint softly stepped toward him. The sand muffled his steps. He reached the man, whose head was still resting on the sand by the dog.

Kneeling, Clint pulled from under his shirt the gifts he had brought for the man—the German textbook, the pencil and paper, the food. He laid them on the sand and touched the man's shoulder.

"Ich bin dein Freund"—I am your friend—I am your friend. The boy struggled to say the strange German words.

Startled, the man leaped up and away from the boy.

54

Desperately the boy said again, *"Ich bin dein Freund."* —I am your friend!

"Freund?" The man looked at the boy. There was such a longing in the man's eyes, the way Mickey's eyes begged for friendship. Then the man took a deep breath. *"Nein, nein."*

He pushed Clint gently away from him and pointed to the sandy road leading to the cottages.

"Nein, nein." Wearily the man turned into his little cave.

"Wait!" called Clint. "Please talk to me. I'll help you! I won't tell anyone who you are. Please, let me help you!"

The man pulled the boards back across the door of his cave, shutting out Clint and Mickey, shutting out the whole world. Clint stared down at the boards, then turned back toward the car. He was desperate. He had to help the man. But he couldn't even talk to him.

Blinded by the sun and heat, Clint kept his head down as he hobbled through the marshy sand. He did not see his father searching for him until he reached the water pump. By then Mr. Jordan had seen Clint and was waiting by the car.

"All I want is a truthful answer, Clint. Where have you been and why did you lie to me?" he asked as the boy looked up, startled. "I came looking for you when you did not come to the pier as you promised. I am very angry because I was worried about you and because you were not honest with me. I want an answer."

Clint looked wearily at his father. Always—always he had told his dad everything. But this time he had promised another man he would not give away his secret. He shook his head. Mr. Jordan stared a long time at the boy's lowered head. Mickey whined around for a loving pat from anybody—anybody at all! No one moved.

"Get in the car, Clint. We're going home. You go to your room until you can give me an answer. I'll get Herbie and the fishing gear."

Quickly Mr. Jordan was back at the car with a very silent Herbie. This was so unusual Clint knew his father must have said something to his brother. Clint hated having Herbie know he was in trouble. He hated it.

When the car stopped at the cottage, Clint hobbled as fast as he could to his room. He fell on his bed and covered his head with the pillow. He had done everything wrong—everything.

8

SAFE WITH HIS DAD

DURING the long afternoon only once did any sound break Clint's thoughts. The voices from the kitchen were loud and angry.

"Honest, Mom, it wasn't me! I never touched those applejacks." Herbie's voice was puzzled.

Mrs. Jordan said, "Well, it certainly wasn't a fish. It had to be you or Clint or maybe even Mickey!"

"Well, it wasn't me."

Clint put his head back under the pillow. Just one more thing he had done wrong.

By the time the smell of frying chicken drifted to Clint's bedroom, he had finished battling with himself. For three hours he had sat on the bed trying to see a way he could help the stranger. But there was no way he could do anything without a grown-up's help. The one grown-up who could help was pretty mad at him right now, but— in all Clint's life his dad had never let him down.

The boy hopped off the bed and limped in search of his father. Clint found him sitting on the steps at the end

57

of the narrow little bridge. Mr. Jordan looked up at the sound of the bare feet hobbling on the bridge.

"Well, Son?" his father asked.

"Dad, you've got to help! I've done everything wrong. I can't think of what to do next, but I promised I'd keep his secret and you've got to promise to keep his secret too! He's all alone—"

"Whoa, there!" Mr. Jordan held up his hand to stop Clint's rush of words. "I'm not asking you to tell a secret. I just want to know why you told me a lie. Why did you run off at the sand hill?"

"But that's it! I was trying to help him by myself—but I can't!" The boy looked up at his dad.

"Clint, start at the beginning—you know, like one, two, three. I guess I must be dumb, but I don't understand at all what you are talking about."

"It's the stranger, Dad—Mr. Weathers' stranger who can't talk. Only he really can talk, but he speaks German, so if he talked, everybody would *know* he is German and put him in a prisoner-of-war camp!"

"What kind of nonsense have you dreamed up now?" Dumbfounded, Mr. Jordan stared at Clint.

"Okay, Dad, here it is in one, two, three. Last summer the Coast Guard caught a German right on the beach in front of Jud's cottage. Right?"

"Right. But he was a spy. The Coast Guard found out he had landed secretly for the purpose of sabotaging the Norfolk Navy Yard," Mr. Jordan said.

"Okay, but the next day Jud and I found that coat, an *extra* coat, didn't we? And the Coast Guard never found anyone else. Right?"

Mr. Jordan listened earnestly as Clint spread out his ideas. A silent stranger suddenly appeared during the winter on the island wearing old and tattered clothes. He did not speak at all. No one knew where he lived, but Clint had found his hideout. And when the boy had hurt his foot, the man did speak a command to Mickey.

"This is hard to believe, Son!"

Clint went on. "Okay, that German book I found. I've said two words to the stranger, *danke*—thank you, and *Freund*—friend. He understood me both times, Dad. But now he's afraid and he's going to leave—I just know he is, Dad. And where can he go?"

"Wait a minute, let me think," said Mr. Jordan. "What a wild thing to happen!"

Suddenly Mr. Jordan hopped up and ran toward the kitchen. To Mrs. Jordan he said, "Quick, Nell, give me that chicken that's already cooked and—uh—some cold milk! Food can help many a problem!"

"Ed, what in the world! Are you crazy? I have supper all ready for us to eat. I'm putting it on the table right now!"

"Well, something's come up. Clint and I have to go. I can't tell you when we'll be back, so just go ahead and eat without us!" Mr. Jordan finished gathering the food and ran out the door.

"Ed, wait!" called Mrs. Jordan. "Where are you going?"

She watched in dismay as Clint and Mr. Jordan hopped into the gray car and sped away with Mickey yipping along behind.

"Dad, you believe me, don't you? And you'll help—

and you won't tell his secret!'' Clint turned to his father as the little car jounced along.

"Son, I just have that old gut feeling that says you're right. And what you say does add up. At least we have to find out who the man is."

The two Jordans popped out of the car at the foot of Jockey's Ridge. Mr. Jordan followed after Clint as the boy and his dog led the way through the marshy patches of sand and saw grass.

"Wait, Dad!" Clint whispered as they came up closer to the sand dune where the hideout was. "How are you going to talk to him?"

"Well, I taught French and German a while in a high school. I ought to be able to talk some with your stranger *if* he is the German you think he is. I just hope he hasn't run away. I know we can help him."

"Oh, Dad—oh!" Clint was so relieved he felt like leaping, but his foot was hurting too much.

"Look, Clint, there's a little light showing through the chinks in those boards. He's there," Mr. Jordan whispered. "I doubt if he's armed, but you let me go first. Stay back."

Flying past the two Jordans, Mickey decided to go first. Jumping up against the boards, the dog yipped to his newfound friend inside. This time the stranger did not move slowly. He flung the boards aside and stared at the boy and his father standing there in the dusk. Mr. Jordan could not tell whether the look on the man's face was one of anger—or fear.

"Freund! Ich bin dein Freund!''—Friend! I am your

friend! Mr. Jordan said in careful German to the man standing in the cave.

He waited anxiously to see what the man would do. He did not expect to hear the harsh sobs that came from the man! Mr. Jordan was stunned. Then he quickly went into the cave and put his hand on the man's shoulder. Slowly in German he began to speak, "We will not hurt you. We will help you. Please tell me, are you German? I promise you will be okay!"

The man's shoulders stopped shaking. He did not lift his head, but he nodded. Very softly he spoke, "Yes, I am German. I must give up. I cannot go on living this way. I am your prisoner."

"My prisoner! But you are not a prisoner. The war ended a year ago. Our soldiers are in your country still, yes, but we are helping your people rebuild. You are not a prisoner," explained Mr. Jordan in his slow German.

The stranger stared at Mr. Jordan. At first his mouth only moved, then he said, "Not a prisoner? The war is over? But what will you do with me? Where will you put me?"

Mr. Jordan looked kindly at the man, "Do with you? Well, I am sure that you will be sent home."

"Home—home—to Germany! To my mother and father—my little brothers!" The man's words tumbled over one another.

Mr. Jordan looked closely at the man. "How old are you?" he asked.

The man smiled thinly. "My birthday was two weeks ago if I've been keeping up with time right. I'm eighteen."

Mr. Jordan sat stunned by the news. "Eighteen—only three years older than Herbie—eighteen!" He sat looking at a young man who looked every bit of thirty. What had this war done?

"I volunteered at sixteen for submarine service. After the basic military training I was shipped out on patrol on a U-boat. We were told how much we could serve our country—what great sailors we would be. But no one told us what life on a U-boat was like. I—I—" Again the young man began to sob in great gulps.

Clint looked angrily at his dad. "What are you saying to him? You promised to help!"

"It's all right, Son, just let him get it all out of his system. You and I have no idea how hard it must have been for a sixteen-year-old to live aboard a U-boat and then hide in a strange country as he has done. I'll tell you all about it. But right now let's take him back to our cottage for the night—if he will go."

He turned to the young German and spoke slowly in the young stranger's language, "Please listen carefully and believe me! You—will—not—be—a—prisoner! You —will—go—home—to—Germany! Please now, go with us to our cottage. I promise, *I promise* you I will help you get home!"

The young man looked up wearily. "Even if I did not trust you, I have no choice. I will go with you."

He stood up in the little cave, touched the cot, straightened the chair. Then he followed Mr. Jordan out into a night where stars were beginning to twinkle. Mr. Jordan let Clint and Mickey lead the way to the little car.

As soon as they reached the cottage, he explained very

62

briefly to a stunned Mrs. Jordan just what the facts were and what she was to do. So far as Clint was concerned, the worst thing she had to do was send him to bed. And his brother had to go too. Herbie was outraged at being treated like a child. But Mr. Jordan said he wanted everybody out of the kitchen, out of the way, and somewhere safe so he didn't have to worry about them—and bed was where he sent them all. You didn't argue with Mr. Jordan when he got like that. Even Mrs. Jordan went to bed!

Clint heard the mumbling voices long into the night until he saw the moon come up and slip across the water to touch his bed. He had done the best he could. He had given his stranger to his dad.

9

TO TOUCH THE LAND

"I'M GOING to let you go with us, Clint, but you must promise not to interfere at all. It will be necessary for the Coast Guard authorities to question Karl, but as I told you, he will not be harmed. He will be returned to Germany." Mr. Jordan looked up at his son.

Clint was standing by the kitchen table, waiting for his father to finish breakfast. He had stared and stared at Karl. His silent stranger had shaved off his old man's beard and had had a bath of sorts. He looked more as if he might have once been young.

Mr. Jordan pushed back his chair. "It's time to go, Karl."

The young German stood up. Turning to Mrs. Jordan, he bobbed his head and said, *"Danke, danke."*

Clint was pretty proud he knew that the word was "thank you" in German. He followed his father and Karl out to the car. Herbie turned to his mother.

"Why couldn't I go, for Pete's sake?" asked Herbie.

"For the same reason I didn't let Clint go on your band

trip. That was your time. This is Clint's. The stranger is his," answered his mother.

"Cripes!" muttered the boy and stomped off around the porch.

Mr. Jordan drove straight to the two-story white Coast Guard Station on the main ocean road. When he asked to see the officer in charge, he was using his superintendent's voice. The young coastguardsman on duty obeyed like any well-behaved schoolboy.

When Mr. Jordan went into another room to see the officer in charge, Clint and Karl stood looking out of the windows facing the sea. Two big white lifeboats were pulled up on the sand. Round life preservers were stacked on the porch facing the ocean. Clint and Karl watched the waves rear up, crash onto the water, and race hissing up the beach. When Mr. Jordan and the Coast Guard officer came into the large airy room, Karl stood stiffly trying to hide his fear.

The officer was saying to Mr. Jordan, "This is the wildest thing I ever heard. If I didn't know you, Mr. Jordan, I really don't think I could even begin to believe you. But after my phone call to Commander Wells in Norfolk, I find there was another case like this out on Long Island. The men there were caught pretty soon, though. This man has been hiding a year!"

He turned to Karl. Sensing the young man's deep fear, he softened his usual military look. "Seaman Karl Schmidt, I would like to talk with you. Mr. Jordan and the boy can come in to my office too."

Mr. Jordan told Karl in German what the officer had said in English. Karl marched stiffly into the office. The three men took chairs around a big desk. Clint stood between his father and his friend.

Mr. Jordan turned to Karl. "I want you to tell this man what you told me last night. Speak slowly now and I will tell him in English what you are saying. And—remember —we are your friends."

Karl looked down at the floor a minute, stiffened his back, then looking straight at the officer, he began in German.

"I did not know why we were sent on patrol this last time. We carried very few torpedoes. Our course was set straight for this coast, it was rumored among the crew. We had a stranger on board, not a Navy man. After a few days off of this coast our commander told us Herr Schulz, the stranger on board, was to go ashore on a special assignment. He asked for a volunteer to take him in the rubber raft."

Karl stopped talking and nervously rubbed his hands together. Mr. Jordan calmly said, "Go on, Karl."

"I—I—volunteered to be the one to row Herr Schulz to shore. It was not because I was brave." He hung his head. "I wanted to touch the land, I wanted to feel the sand. I did not think much about the danger of being caught."

The officer asked him, "What was Herr Schulz to do after he landed?"

Karl answered, "I was told nothing. I did hear the Navy yards talked of. But I only was to row him ashore, hide for twenty-four hours, and row him back to the U-boat. If he did not come back after the twenty-four hours, I was to go back to the U-boat alone. But I feel sure we were swept too far along the shore by the strong tide. We were supposed to land at a lonely stretch of dunes which our commander had sighted through the periscope during the daylight hours. But when we landed we were right in front of a row of cottages, and the men on horseback discovered Herr Schulz immediately. I think they did not see me. I had gone up to the dunes to find a hiding place for myself during the daylight hours to come. I was behind a dune when the men found Herr Schulz and the rubber raft. I took off my sailor's coat and hid it in the sand, hoping my undershirt would be more like ordinary clothes."

When his father told in English what Karl had said in German, Clint said excitedly, "Yes, yes, that's the one Jud and I found last summer, Dad!"

"Quiet, Son!" Mr. Jordan spoke sharply.

"You must have been only about sixteen when you joined the Navy, weren't you?" asked the Coast Guard officer.

"They let sixteen-year-olds volunteer as the war went on. We learned after we got on the U-boat that they let us greenhorns on because they had lost so many men and subs. That first patrol out made us want to climb overboard and jump into the sea. We were all seasick at first. We lay wretched on our bunks, longing only to die." The young German tumbled over his words now in the memory of those awful days. "When we got over our seasickness, things were a little better. But at the beginning of every patrol it was terrifying to be confined in a U-boat.

Supplies were stored everywhere so you could not even sit up straight to eat. It was possible only to stretch out on the bunks.

"Hammocks holding supplies were hung overhead everywhere. Hard navy bread, called *Kommissbrot,* and potatoes were stored under the narrow eating tables so you could not put your knees under. We sat on extra torpedoes piled where we ate. All of our spare time we spent on our bunks, talking with our friends or sometimes playing chess.

"When the fresh supplies were all used up and we had *some* room to move in, we had only canned food to eat. And the fresh water was strictly rationed so that it would last until the end of the patrol.

"The U-boat was in constant motion—corkscrewing, pitching, yawing, rolling. We breathed stale, stink-laden air. We had half the amount of sleep men needed. And always, always the fear of every early evening when we had to surface to recharge our batteries. If we were sighted then by an enemy destroyer, we could expect a carpet of depth charges laid over us as we quickly submerged. Sometimes all the lights would go out and we would cling to anything as charges exploded around us in the blackness.

"And there was always the monotony—no difference between day and night. The lights had to be burning all the time. There was no difference between weekdays and Sundays—only you wore a clean shirt on Sundays if you still had one!" Karl grinned at this thought. "Sometimes the captain let us seamen look out of the periscope. We have seen children playing on the shore in the daytime.

We have seen horses moving along the sand, but I stopped taking my turn to see the shore. Looking out of the periscope at that kind of life and then turning back to the sweaty insides of our U-boat home, I could not stand to see outside anymore.

"When the chance came to get ashore—even on the enemy's shore—" The young man nodded, embarrassed. "Well, I was the first to volunteer. I did not care what happened! I did not know I would spend a year talking to no one, eating boiled seaweed because I could not find food. I even wanted to be back on the U-boat to hear a German word."

Then he looked at Clint. "The boy said the first German words I heard in a year. He said *danke* and *Freund. Meinen Freund.*" The young man touched Clint's arm.

A great roar sounded outside the Coast Guard Station. Clint ran to the window and saw a helicopter landing right outside on the large black-tarred parking space. Karl was half out of his chair in fright. The Coast Guard officer touched the young German's shoulder.

"It's all right," he said. "This is the helicopter that will take you to the Navy headquarters in Norfolk. You will be all right. I promise you."

Clint and his father stood on the wide porch of the Coast Guard Station and watched Karl climb into the helicopter. The whirring blades of the aircraft lifted the helicopter up. As long as they could see each other, Karl and Clint waved.

10

X MARKED THE SPOT

"I DON'T SEE how one family can have so much junk!" fussed Mr. Jordan. The July day had hardly begun and Mr. Jordan was already sweating. He rumpled his hair as he tried to figure out where in the gray car he could put the pile of stuff sitting on the sand.

"I know we did not bring all this with us! Everybody will just have to get rid of something!"

The angrier he became the redder his face grew. Mrs. Jordan grinned and patted him on the shoulder.

She said, "You say that every summer."

Two hours later Mr. Jordan had wedged the last paper bag in and tied on the last suitcase. Brushing the sand from his hands, he called to Mrs. Jordan, "Nell, get the boys in the car. I want to get back home before dark tonight."

Herbie trailed lazily down the narrow bridge. Mrs. Jordan bustled around checking locked windows and doors of the old cottage. Hurrying to the car, she said, "Everything's done—it's clean and locked. We can go now, but, oh, I hate for July to be over. This year has been exciting but still a good rest."

She settled herself comfortably in the front seat, trying to find a spot for her feet between the picnic basket and the jug of ice water.

"Well, I'm not going," said Mr. Jordan.

"What! Why, Ed, what do you mean?"

"Because you've left our younger son, that's why. Where's Clint?"

Mrs. Jordan turned to look at the back. Herbie and Mickey sat wilted in the heat of the car, but there was no Clint squashed in between everything else.

"Herbie," she commanded, "go find that boy! I told him we were leaving. I thought he was already in the car."

Herbie climbed out of the back seat in great disgust and stomped off across the long narrow bridge. He searched all around the porch and still found no Clint.

Standing by the back steps, he called, "Clint, where are you? Are you locked inside?"

"No," a low voice answered above him. Herbie looked up and saw his brother sprawled on the outhouse roof, staring into the water. Clint spat down into the water to see if he could hit a stick drifting by. Missed. Herbie spat and hit the wood dead center. He looked up at his brother again. Clint didn't even blink.

"What are you daydreaming about, Clint? Your old stranger?" Herbie looked at his brother with the teeniest bit of understanding in his eyes.

"I just wish I could know what happened to him after he left. Ten whole days and we don't know a thing.

Whoosh! Up he went in that helicopter and not a word since. How do I know where he is? How do I know they've been nice to him?"

"The war is over. They told you he could go to his home. He's not rotting in any old prisoner-of-war camp. They don't even have them anymore." Herbie tried to reason with Clint. "But come on now. Mom's gonna get mad as heck if you don't hurry up!"

Clint climbed slowly down the post to the porch and stood looking out across the Albemarle Sound. "Well, I guess it was the best July we've ever had anyway."

He followed Herbie out to the car. After everybody's grumbling efforts to get settled, Clint turned his face to the back window to watch the last minutes of Jackson cottage. The little gray car went down the road toward the post office.

Mr. Jordan couldn't persuade anybody to go inside for a last good-by. He went in alone to return the cottage key to Mr. Weathers. In a few minutes he was back on the big porch. Waving his arm, he called, "Everybody inside right now! You, too, Nell!"

Puzzled, the family climbed out of the car and up the steps. Inside the big dim room Mr. Weathers was waiting for them, standing with his hands behind his back. When all the Jordans were lined up in front of him, he looked at Clint.

"Well, old friend, you sure shook up the island this summer! Here we had a mystery staring us right in the face, and it took you and that black dog of yours to figure it out! You oughta be pretty proud of yourself!"

"Naw." Clint squirmed.

"Well, I think I've got something you've been waiting for, seeing as how you asked me about the mail every day for the last ten days!" He handed Clint a bulky brown envelope.

Clint tore into the package. He pulled out a bundle of newspapers wrapped around something. With everybody crowding around him, he carefully unrolled the papers. There in the middle was a tiny wooden black dog, carved to the exact likeness of Mickey. A little white sign hung around his neck: *"Für meinen treuen Freund,"* and below the German words carefully printed in English, "For my true friend from Karl."

"Oh, golly!" breathed Clint. "I'll never, never let this go!"

"Let me see!" Herbie grabbed for the carving.

"Watch out!" Clint yelled, holding on to his gift.

Mr. Weathers leaned over to look carefully. "I'll bet the stranger carved that out of the trees growing near his cave. Looks just like that kind of wood. But I have something else for you, Mr. Clint!" And with great dignity and a deep bow he handed a long white envelope to Clint.

The boy stared at the address in the left-hand corner of the envelope: Secretary of the Navy, United States of America! And the letter was addressed to Mr. Clint Jordan, c/o Postmaster, Nags Head, N.C.

Slowly he opened the letter and read aloud:

"Dear Clint,

"When a war is over and the differences between countries are being settled, it is difficult to repair the broken bonds of friendship. But you have shown the way by extending the hand of kindness to a very lonely and very scared young man.

"I thought you would like to know that your friend, Karl, left yesterday for his home in Heidelberg, Germany. He asked me to mail to you a small carving of your dog. I gave him your address in the town where you and your family live. Karl plans to write to you when he is home again.

"Clint, the Department of the Navy would be honored to have you, your father, and one friend of your choice to be our guests at the Norfolk Navy Yard on the last Friday in August. We would like to show you some of the ships that fought so valiantly in the war. We thought you might like to have lunch aboard one of the submarines so that you might see how your friend, Karl, lived.

"We hope to hear from you soon saying you will come."

And it was signed by the Secretary of the Navy himself! Herbie breathed a big, "Wow!"

"My goodness!" exclaimed Mrs. Jordan.

"Well." Mr. Jordan beamed. "Which friend do you want to take? Jud, I suppose?"

Clint stood staring at the letter in his hand. With his head still down he said, "No—not Jud. I—I—I want Herbie." He looked up quickly at his brother.

"Me! Uh, I mean—me?" Herbie's voice squeaked from little boy to grown man all in the same sentence. "Well, I guess I can go—I don't guess I'll be too busy."

Mr. Jordan just smiled. Herbie socked Clint on the

shoulder. Clint socked Herbie on the shoulder and grinned.

After a last salute from Mr. Weathers to Clint, they all piled into the car.

"This calls for a celebration!" said Mr. Jordan. "We'll stop at that little place to eat near the bridge across the Sound. I'm going to have a popcorn sandwich and some magnolia pie!"

Clint exploded with laughter.

Herbie very seriously said, "I'll have a harmonica hot dog with onions."

Mrs. Jordan, very dignified, said, "I'll have fish pancakes with seawater syrup."

And the little gray car rocked down the sandy highway.